Sprout

Sprout is the tale of a succulent who is all grown up and is faced with the decision of leaving his friends and family. Sprout is an easy read for children of all ages to help introduce the idea of growing up and make big life transitions a little easier.

Once upon a time, in a garden far far away, lived a little succulent named Sprout.

Sprout lived in a beautiful garden with
all of his friends.

For as long as Sprout could remember he
had lived in the garden.

It was the only home Sprout ever knew.

Sprout loved his home. He had so many friends
in the garden, as far as the eye could see...

But only a few plants in the garden were
Sprouts true friends.

Sprout talked with his friends every day.

Sprouts favorite thing to do with his friends was to hang out in the sun.

Sprout loved his life in the garden, he got all of
the sun and water any plant could ever ask for.

Everything seemed great for Sprout...until one day things started to change.

The air was different and
Sprout noticed.

Weeks went by with Sprout feeling different.

One day, Sprout noticed two little legs
start to grow out of the bottom of his pot.

As more time passed, Sprout and his legs grew more.

After some time, Sprout realized it was time for
him to leave the garden.

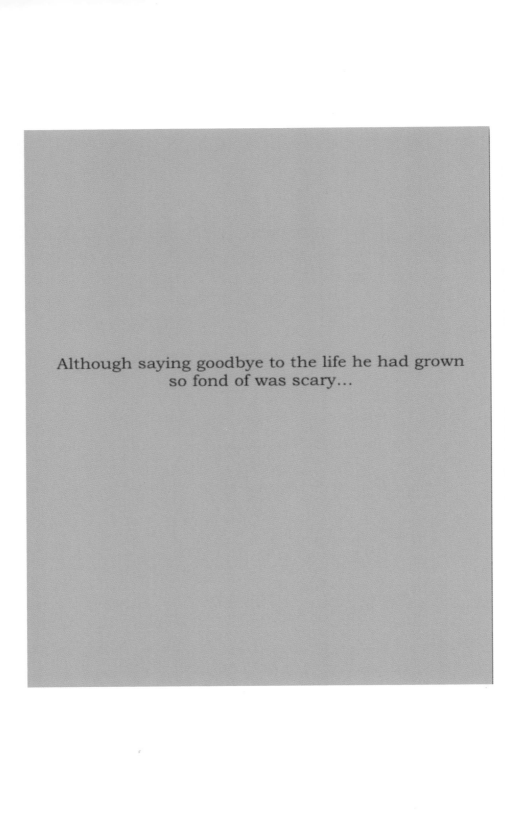

Although saying goodbye to the life he had grown
so fond of was scary...

Sprout realized he had grown, not just legs, but he had grown up.

It was now time for Sprout to close one chapter of
his life and start another.

The hardest part of moving on was
saying goodbye.

Sprout said goodbye to all of his friends, and
left the garden.

Sprout looked back only once as he left...

...to say goodbye to his past self.

Although growing up and moving on can be scary, sometimes you can't help but grow legs!

The end.

Printed in Great Britain
by Amazon

14913759R00016